THE KING'S DRAPES

atmosphere press

Each day the king inspected his castle
drapes and proclaimed:

I am the king, and the King makes the rules.
Here ye! Here ye! These drapes will not do.
Change them! Change them!
I must have brand new.

The king's court
scrambled with
fine cloth and
thread
To stitch, sew
and hang new
drapes instead.

But, alas! Every day the king would repeat his claim:

I am the king, and the king makes the rules.
Here ye! Here ye! These drapes will not do.
Change them! Change them!
I must have brand new.

So much time and fine fabric was waste
on the cruel king's demands.
Meanwhile, the people of the land wor
old tattered rags.

ill, day after day, the selfish king hollered the same:
I am the king, and the king makes the rules.
Here ye! Here ye! These drapes will not do.
Change them! Change them!
I must have brand new.

Soon, there was no cloth left, and all in the king's court were frozen with fright. What would they tell the king? He expected new drapes be sewn every night!

With nothing left but scraps
to sew,
The king went to sleep and
the whole court went home.

They went back to their families and back to their lives.
They told tales of the king's drapes to their children, husbands and wives.

But the most clever young girl in all the land
Heard these tales and decided she must lend a hand.

The girl made a plan both bold and brave.
After all, **she** had a kingdom to save.

She traveled to the castle the very next morning.
She marched up to the gates without any warning.

The girl told the ruler, "On this special day, your highness,
The windows of the castle need neither dressing nor fineness.

Today the sun will shine in the room like gold. It will be grand and magnificent to behold."

"No drapes?" thought the King.
"What a bore!"
Though he was quite tempted by the allure.

The king considered a moment and then made his decision:
"There shall be no drapes to block this royal vision!"

With windows undressed, the King stood
in his usual spot
Where once there were drapes, but now
there were not.

The king stared through the windows and could now see
The people of the kingdom had grown poor as could be.

Sadness befell the stubborn old king. "What have I done, always demanding new things?"

The old drapes! Pull them out!" the king exclaimed.
I've taken more than my share and I am ashamed."

Day turned into night and night into day
As the king and his court stitched away.

hey made the finest pants and shirts.
hey made jackets, hats, scarves and skirts.

The young girl checked in on the work in full swing.
She smiled with pride. Her plan was working.

Throughout the land, the clothing was shared.
The King had changed and now declared:
  I, the King, took advantage of the rules.
  You deserve better than I've put you through.
  Change your clothes! Change your clothes!
  I helped make you brand new.

The king learned a lesson important to all, far and wide.
Greed takes away more than it can ever provide.

About Atmosphere Press

Atmosphere Press is an independent, full-service publisher for excellent books in all genres and for all audiences. Learn more about what we do at atmospherepress.com.

We encourage you to check out some of Atmosphere's latest children's releases, which are available at Amazon.com and via order from your local bookstore:

Young Yogi and the Mind Monsters, by Sonja Radvila
Buried Treasure, a picture book by Anne Krebbs
The Magpie and The Turtle, a Native American-inspired folk tale by Timothy Yeahquo, Jr.
The Alligator Wrestler: A Girls Can Do Anything Book, by Carmen Petro
My WILD First Day of School, a picture book by Dennis Mathew
I Will Love You Forever and Always, a picture book by Sarah M. Thomas Mariano
The Sky Belongs to the Dreamers, a picture book by J.P. Hostetler
Shooting Stars, A Girls Can Do Anything Book, by Carmen Petro
Carpenters and Catapults, A Girls Can Do Anything Book, by Carmen Petro
Gone Fishing, A Girls Can Do Anything Book, by Carmen Petro
Owlfred the Owl Learns to Fly, a picture book by Caleb Foster
Bello the Cello, a picture book by Dennis Mathew
That Scarlett Bacon, a picture book by Mark Johnson

About the Author

Jocelyn Tambascio is insatiable in her desire to learn. When she isn't reading, she is bingeing podcasts, or trying to decipher a mystery before the solution is revealed. Commensurate with her love of learning, she is a Doctor of Education with over twenty years of experience working in the field of human exceptionalities.

Jocelyn's loving husband, Steven, beautiful stepchildren, Aiden and Kiley, and incredible nieces, Phoenix and Storm, were all inspirational to The King's Drapes.

About the Illustrator

Jen Born always assumed she'd have to be walking around this world with a briefcase wearing fancy grown-up clothes by the age of 37. She thanks her lucky stars that she has found success being exactly who she is-quirky, artsy and a little bit weird. Living as a full time artist and running her own business, PS Enjoy Your Life, since 2009 has brought her much happiness, but illustrating this book tops the list.

She lives in a bright yellow house on a tree-lined street in Rochester, NY with her wonderful wife, Carey, dog, Tully, and cat, Patch.

Her biggest dream is to one day read this story to her own children.

CPSIA information can be obtained
at www.ICGtesting.com
Printed in the USA
LVHW011753121120
671498LV00007B/268

9 781649 21882